BEHIND
THE
BLOODLINES
A DONATI BLOODLINES COMPANION

BETHANY-KRIS

Published by Bethany-Kris

www.bethanykris.com

eISBN 13: 978-1-988197-34-0

Print ISBN 13: 978-1-988197-41-8

Cover Art © Jay Aheer

DEDICATION

For all the lovers of Calisto and Emma.

CONTENTS

DONATI DELETED FILES..7

CHAPTER ONE..8

CHAPTER TWO..16

CHAPTER THREE..28

DONATI EXTENDED FILE..42

CHAPTER FOUR..43

DONATI UNSEEN FILES..51

CHAPTER FIVE..52

CHAPTER SIX..58

CHAPTER SEVEN..76

CHAPTER EIGHT..92

CHAPTER NINE..108

DONATI OTHER POV FILES..121

CHAPTER TEN..122

CHAPTER ELEVEN..132

DONATI
DELETED FILES

I.
DONATI
DELETED FILES #1

The Loss

Author's Note: This deleted scene takes place at the end of book one, *Thin Lies*. It was the one and only scene deleted from the book, as it was not how I wanted to end the first book.

Emma paced the length of the master bathroom. The sweat on her palms made her skin both chilled and sticky. She wiped her hands off on her dress for the fifth time since her pacing had started. It was a good distraction, if nothing else.

It kept Emma from checking the long, thin piece of plastic sitting on the counter.

The time had already passed.

8

Three *extra* minutes, to be exact.

She still couldn't check.

Emma didn't really need to look because she already knew what the simple, drugstore pregnancy test would say. Her menstrual cycle had never been late before. Not one single time in her life.

She was officially two days late.

Perhaps, she could've attributed her late period to the stress of her current circumstances. She was certainly stressed enough for it, what with her arranged marriage, new husband, and her entire life being turned upside down.

Emma knew—somehow—the stress wasn't the cause.

She had faced stress before.

Never was she late.

Emma knew what that meant. She was pregnant. Which would, of course, make her new husband happy. Over the moon, even. That was, if Emma could manage to convince Affonso it was his child she was carrying.

Because it wasn't Affonso's baby.

It was Calisto's.

Emma wasn't a stupid woman, despite what her current situation implied about her ability to make good choices. She could do basic math, and understood how her cycle worked.

If her cycle was only a couple of days late, she would have conceived at least two weeks prior. She was newly married, by just a few days, to be exact, and Affonso had not touched her once before they married.

Emma was still able to count back the days easily enough. To right about the time she and Cal had spent a whole night and subsequent morning fucking.

Her husband's *nephew*.

Emma caught sight of her reflection in the bathroom mirror.

Wary.

Tired.

Worried.

Unsure.

Pregnant.

How could you be so stupid?

You knew better.

Well, what did it matter now?

It didn't, she decided.

Emma stepped forward and plucked the pregnancy test off the counter, checking the windows for what she already knew. Two bright, thick pink lines stared back at her.

So. Fucking. Pregnant.

Emma looked at her reflection again.

She would do what she had to.

She would lie.

Whatever it took to make her husband believe this child was his.

Emma stuffed the pregnancy test in her pocket, determined to destroy it. She could afford a week, or maybe even two, before she would tell Affonso.

It wasn't a perfect plan.

But it was something.

Emma found Affonso in his office, sipping coffee and reading from a newspaper. It was the same thing he did every morning, and he preferred not to be interrupted while he did it.

On this morning, she didn't think that he would mind.

It'd been a week since she stood in the bathroom, panicking, as she stared at a pregnancy test. There was a part of Emma, a very small part that spent the week praying and hoping for some kind of damn miracle.

Foolishly, she only thought of Calisto.

That maybe, like a white knight, he would roll through and save the day. He would save Emma.

It was nothing more than a silly, stupid thought that would never come true. Calisto hadn't even been around since the wedding. He had clearly drawn his lines in the sand, and he was on one side, while Emma was firmly stuck on the other.

She had to do what she had to do, now.

Calisto would understand, surely.

If he ever found out …

Emma didn't think that Calisto would ever learn the truth. After all, her very life depended on making sure no one knew what happened between her and

Cal. Never mind, making sure everyone believed Affonso was her child's father.

There was no other option for Emma except for what she was about to do.

"Can I help you, Emma?"

Affonso's cool, yet irritated tone, broke Emma from her inner thoughts. He stared hard at her from behind his large desk, clearly annoyed at her presence.

Emma had learned a few things about her new husband and his expectations for her, rather fast.

He only wanted to hear, look, or speak to her when he wanted to. She was better appreciated at a distance. She was, in every sense, his trophy wife.

"Um." Emma wrung her hands, avoiding Affonso stare. "Do you have a minute?"

"I have many minutes. That doesn't mean I'm willing to share them."

Emma had also learned that the only time she could expect patience and a soft hand from her husband was when he wanted to fuck her. She had been terrified on their wedding night, knowing that refusing to sleep with Affonso would do her no good. It was not that he was older, or unattractive, because

13

he wasn't. She simply could not enjoy sex with a man she despised.

But he never hurt her during sex. He was careful. He did expect her participation, to some extent. Emma was grateful that, at the very least, he did not force her.

"Emma," Affonso said, "what is it?"

A large part of her wanted to stay silent.

The small part of her that knew it was better to speak up, won.

"I'm pregnant," Emma blurted.

She pulled a pregnancy test from the pocket of her jeans, a new one she'd taken just before finding her husband. Affonso's eye caught the test and his smile grew.

A genuine, joyous smile.

Emma swallowed back the guilt and shame chewing her alive inside. "Are you happy?"

Joy danced in Affonso's eyes. "So happy."

Well, then.

Emma had done her job.

For as happy as her husband seemed in that moment, Emma never thought that only a couple of weeks later, as she was rendered immobile in her own blood on the kitchen floor, Affonso would be sickened at the sight of her.

He would not care that she was bleeding.

He would not understand her tears at losing the baby.

He would not be kind at all.

She knew none of those things.

Until the loss came.

2.
DONATI
DELETED FILES #2

Missing

Author's Note: This scene was removed from the end of book two, *Thin Lines*, as I felt better ending the book how I did, and allowing the *new* Calisto to speak first at the beginning of book three.

Calisto was surprised to see his uncle's wife sitting in the library in front of the grand piano. She wasn't playing the instrument, but rather, drifting her fingers over the lid covering the keys.

She rarely ever came into the library, and he would know, as it was where he spent ninety percent of his time. Well, when he wasn't at another doctor's appointment or doing another round of therapy.

The library, and the piano, was a reprieve of sorts for Calisto. He didn't have to think about his shattered shoulder, his broken femur, the wheelchair he was still constantly stuck in, or his messed up mind.

His mind that was ... missing.

He thought—maybe—he wouldn't care about the rest of his injuries or problems, if only his mind would work again. If only he could remember what was lost to him.

Calisto was grateful for his uncle, and the way Affonso had brought him into his home to recover from the accident. But nothing felt quite right. Sometimes, everything just seemed off. Even when everyone was smiling at him, Calisto felt like they were lying to him somehow.

Nonsense, he thought. Or rather, that was what he was often told. Whenever he brought up his odd feelings to his uncle, Affonso brushed it off, claiming that it was nothing more than Calisto's lack of knowledge playing tricks on him. That perhaps the trauma of his accident, and what he was subconsciously remembering of it, was bleeding into the conscious side of his brain.

Calisto hated how that made sense; hated, even, how he clung onto the idea, wanting it to be the truth.

He didn't understand why he felt *that* way, either.

He had no reason to be distrustful of the people around him, especially his uncle. Yet, those thoughts and feelings were still very present.

Constantly.

Persistent.

Demanding.

A soft sigh broke Calisto from the prison that had become his thoughts. It took him all of ten seconds to realize where he was again, what he was doing there, and what was happening around him.

In the library entrance, stuck in his wheelchair. He'd found Emma sitting at the piano, but not playing.

Nothing was wrong.

Everything was fine.

Relax, he told himself.

The zoning out thing had become far too common, and therefore, a problem. Calisto could be doing anything, at any random time of the day or night, and suddenly be pulled into his thoughts, lost to a trance-like state to his own mind. The doctors said it was normal, considering his traumatic brain injury, and the subsequent stress of having amnesia didn't help. It was like his brain's way of blocking out all of the unneeded background noise, and simply focusing on what was immediately at hand.

Calisto didn't care *why*.

He just wanted it to *stop*.

Albeit annoyed about zoning out, Calisto was grateful to be brought out of his daze. He found Emma was still sitting at the piano like he had first found her, seemingly unaware of his presence behind her.

There was something in the shadow of her profile, an emotion that she couldn't quite hide.

Longing.

And sadness.

Both were there.

He felt terrible for spying on her. After all, it had been him who snapped at her a while ago for sneaking up on him while he was in that very same spot.

Calisto decided to make his presence known. "Do you play, Emma?"

For a split second, Calisto swore he saw Emma's back tense. She shot him a look over her shoulder. That sadness and longing disappeared from her features, a false happiness taking its place.

She could smile all she wanted, Calisto decided, but there was clearly something inside of Emma Donati that was deeply unhappy.

"I do," Emma replied, "but not nearly as well as you."

Calisto scoffed, smiling at the same time. "That can't be true."

He rolled himself further into the room.

Emma turned back to the piano. "Oh, it's true. I'm technically trained, but that means nothing when I don't have the right ear for it."

Strangely, Calisto understood what she meant.

"Well, you must like it enough. You certainly stare at the piano like it's holding all sorts of secrets for you."

Again, Emma tensed. "Maybe it does. Who

knows?"

He fully believed that she knew.

Entirely.

"Care to share one?" Calisto asked.

Emma's eyes widened as Calisto's wheelchair came to a stop beside the piano bench. "Share what?"

"A secret."

A nervous burst of laughter fell from her pink lips. "You're being funny now. Where's Affonso? Weren't you supposed to go to that dinner with him?"

Calisto shrugged. "That was two hours ago. I changed my mind."

"Oh."

"And you're deflecting."

Emma's gaze darted away. "You should let people have their secrets, Cal. There's usually a good reason for them."

"Maybe so."

"I hear a *but* in there."

"But," Calisto said, smirking, "you could indulge me."

"That's an interesting way to try and convince me."

He waved at his chair, his one constant companion and enemy. "Yes, indulge me. This is all the fun I get in a day, wheeling from one room to the other."

"Besides," Calisto added, "we don't really know each other that well. This could help."

He saw that flash of sadness come back in Emma's eyes at his words, but it disappeared before he could think on it for too long.

"I don't have secrets," Emma said.

"Bullshit."

Her mouth popped open. "Pardon?"

"Bull*shit*, Emma. Everyone has secrets. It's a part of being human. And, you can't tell me that a woman of your age, arranged to marry a man of my uncle's age, doesn't have at least one secret locked up tight."

Emma's lips pressed tightly together, like she was trying to hold the words back. "Fine, then. I don't have secrets I am *willing* to share."

"That's no fun."

"You should have known better than to ask, Cal."

"Maybe, but if I don't try, then I will never know

22

the what ifs."

Emma lifted a single shoulder. "I'm not allowed to have secrets. Not in this life, living in this house, married to that man. Secrets are dangerous."

Calisto nodded, understanding that, at least. "You should know, Emma, that sometimes you don't have to speak to tell your secrets. Your face tells them all. In case you didn't already know."

She smiled, but the sight was sad. "Is that so?"

"It is, at least when you think people aren't watching. Then, you wear your emotions clearly, unhidden on your face, like your heart is on your sleeve. Especially your unhappiness."

Emma didn't look the least bit surprised at Calisto's statement. "Someone has already told me that at one time. I guess you can say I haven't gotten any better at fixing the problem."

"Is it really your problem to fix?"

"Huh?"

"Your unhappiness that you try to hide," Calisto clarified. "Is that your problem to fix, if you're not the one causing it?"

Emma laughed. "Calisto, I am always the one left

causing my own unhappiness."

"What would make you happy?"

This time, Emma's smile was bright and genuine as she turned it on him. "Right now, hearing you play the piano would be great."

Calisto could do that.

And if it helped to make Emma look a little less sad, then he would count that as a win in his book.

Emma got up from the bench and moved it out of the way, allowing Calisto to wheel his chair into the proper position. Sitting in front of the piano, and lifting the lid from the keys, he found his calm and comforting place again. A small piece of his life that was sure and certain, it was perfectly familiar. Perhaps that was why he kept coming back to the piano day after day to play, no matter his mood.

Emma sat off to the side, patiently on the bench, waiting for him to start. Her hands rested atop the small swell of her stomach, a smile playing at the edges of her lips.

"Ready?" Calisto asked.

"Always, Cal."

How often had he played for her before his

accident?

Calisto chose not to ask.

Instead, he got lost in the comfort and grounding familiarity the piano provided. For the subsequent half of an hour that followed, was the melody that his fingers helped his mind to create with the piano keys. All the while, Emma never once spoke.

It was only once Calisto had stopped playing entirely, that he looked over to see Emma beaming down at her tiny swell. Her hands had moved lower on her stomach, her fingers tapping a beat over her dress.

"He likes that," Emma said.

"He?"

"The baby. He likes the music, I think."

Calisto's gaze dropped to Emma's stomach again, and the strangest urge swept through him. He wanted to touch her swelled stomach, feel the movement of the child she spoke so lovingly about, and understand the one thing that clearly made her so happy. Especially when it seemed like so little provided her with that joy.

"I didn't know the baby was a boy," Calisto said.

Emma shrugged. "I had some early tests done. Genetics gave the gender away."

Before Calisto knew what was happening, or he could stop himself, he had turned his chair and wheeled closer to Emma. Hesitantly, he held out a hand.

"Could I feel?"

Emma didn't even think about it, simply took his hand and placed it where hers had previously been on her stomach. A second passed with no movement, and then a few more. Calisto was sure that he had missed the chance to feel the unborn baby moving to his music.

Then, he felt it.

Something thumping gently against his fingertips before it went away. Maybe *thumping* wasn't the right word to use. It felt more like a bubble bursting beneath the taut roundness of Emma's stomach.

And then there it was again.

And *again*.

Calisto let out a heavy breath. "Wow."

"It's the most amazing—"

Emma's words cut off as a door slammed. The

front door. Like a bolt of lightning had struck under her feet, Emma was up off the bench, had pushed Calisto's hand away, and glanced at the library door.

"One more secret for the hell of it," Emma said, "but this time, we can both share it."

"Huh?" Calisto looked up at her.

Emma's face had reverted to stone, no unhappiness to be found, but no emotion, either. "This never happened."

Calisto didn't get a chance to respond.

Emma was already leaving him behind.

What was he missing?

3.
DONATI
DELETED FILES #3

The Last Visit

Author's Note: This deleted scene takes place at the end of book three, *Thin Lives*, before the Epilogue, about three or so months after the wedding. It was not included in that final chapter, because I wanted only a happy, joyous feeling to those ending bits after all the angst. And the Sorrento family does not exhibit those emotions, especially here.

Emma's discomfort was not going unnoticed by her husband, as their private jet taxied down the runway. Although he was supposed to stay seated until the plane came to a complete stop, she heard the clink of metal before Calisto moved closer to her. She relaxed instantly when his lips pressed softly to her temple.

"You okay?"

"Nervous," Emma answered honestly.

Calisto kissed her again. "It'll be fine, *bella*."

"I know."

Awkward

Uncomfortable.

Probably irritating.

But it *would* be okay by the end of her visit to her mother and father.

After all, it wasn't like she would be permanently staying, and she couldn't be forced to do anything that she didn't want to do while she was in Vegas. She found all of those things very reassuring.

Emma was not the same woman she had been the last time she was in Las Vegas, never mind in the presence of her family. She was entirely different. Married, divorced, a mother, and a married woman again.

But these same details that made her a different person, also worried her, especially where her mother and father were concerned. They were not the kind of people who cared about the semantics of circumstance, or a person's happiness. They cared about appearance.

They had only ever cared for how they looked to others.

Their public image.

Very little else mattered to George and Minnie Sorrento.

How would Emma, as a divorced Catholic, remarried to her previous husband's nephew, with a child on her hip, make her parents look?

Not well at all.

She had done what her parents demanded of her, when they demanded it. She married the man they chose, when they chose him. She hadn't fought them on it. She could not help the events that followed, leading her to where she was now.

Happy.

Loved.

Protected.

Content.

Adored.

"We can always get this plane back up into the air," Calisto said. "It just needs a quick refueling stop."

Emma sighed. "No, it's fine."

"Is it?"

"They're my parents," Emma said. "They're Cross's grandparents. He deserves to know them, doesn't he?"

Calisto and Emma looked to their sleeping son just across the aisle. The plane ride had not bothered him at all. He didn't even wake up when the plane touched down on the tarmac. Emma swore her son could sleep through a hurricane.

In that moment, she was grateful.

"Do you think that they really care if they have a grandchild?"

Emma frowned. "No."

"Then let's not use Cross as an excuse to do this, Emmy."

"It's me," Emma said quietly. "I'm just feeling off."

Calisto nodded once. "Okay, then. You say the word, and we will go. Anytime. Got it?"

"Yeah, Cal. I got it."

She knew he meant every word, too.

Emma loved him even more for it.

"Emma!"

The high-pitched—too high, false, and practiced—greeting from her mother, made Emma cringe. She managed to hide her reaction just in time to accept a half-hearted hug from Minnie.

"Ma," Emma greeted. "How have you been?"

Minnie waved a hand high. "Busy, the usual."

Emma wasn't the least bit surprised when her mother didn't return the sentiment by asking how *she* was. Minnie had only really cared for her own happiness, after all. Others joy did not matter, never mind a lack thereof.

Calisto caught Emma's eye, and for a second, his cool mask slipped as he offered her a reassuring smile. Little Cross sat happily awake in his father's arms, his wide eyes, innocent and curious, locked on the new person in his small world. His grandmother.

"Ma," Emma said, directing Minnie toward her husband and son, "this is Cross. And you remember Calisto, I'm sure."

Minnie flashed Calisto with a smile, and barely gave her grandson any attention at all.

"Of course," Minnie replied. "How far you have climbed since last we saw one another, Calisto."

Emma saw the flash of annoyance in Calisto's gaze, but he hid it well enough. He chose his next words carefully, Emma noticed.

"Sometimes, that's just how this life works out for us," Calisto said.

Minnie pursed her lips, an amused glint in her eye as she glanced between Emma and Calisto. "Yes, I'm sure."

Calisto didn't bother to respond to that.

Neither did Emma.

"Gamma."

Cross's sudden babble, a word that Emma had been working with him all week to say—Grandma—finally drew in Minnie's gaze. She smiled tersely at the baby, as though she had no patience or interest in his chatter, or his curiosity in her.

"Cute," she drawled, "but I am much too young and pretty for that child to be calling me grandma."

That child.

Both Calisto and Emma stiffened on the spot.

Cross, on the other hand, pointed at Minnie, unaware and uncaring about her annoyance at him.

"Gamma," he said firmer, wanting confirmation that he had gotten the word, and the person, right.

"Yes," Emma assured her son, hoping it would be enough to quiet him. "That's Grandma, Cross."

"God, Emma."

She ignored her mother.

Calisto gave Emma a wink. "I think he needs a diaper change." He passed Minnie a look, adding, "I'll just give you two a minute."

Once Calisto had disappeared down the mansion hallway, Emma turned back on her mother. She tried goddamn hard not to show her anger at having her own mother outright dismiss her son, and failed miserably.

"You could at least smile at Cross," Emma said.

"Wave. Say hi. Or *something*. He's a baby, Ma. He doesn't understand why *you* don't want him to call you his grandma."

Minnie shrugged. "He'll learn."

Emma had all she could do not to slap her mother. It wouldn't have done her any good, and that was probably the one and only reason why she held the urge back.

He'll learn.

How silly and stupid that sounded.

Yet, at the same time, Emma knew her mother absolutely believed it, too. It had been the same lesson, in theory, that Emma had been forced to learn as she grew up with Minnie as her mother.

She was only for show.

Happiness could be bought.

And faked.

She had probably only been born to her parents because it had been the right thing to do for their image, not because they actually wanted children.

"You're his only grandmother," Emma said quietly.

Calisto's mother was dead. Cross had literally no

one else to fill that spot in his life. For the once a year—or less, likely—meetings the Sorrento and Donati families would have, couldn't Minnie at least *pretend* to give a shit?

Apparently not.

"So?" Minnie asked.

Emma had her answer.

She still wasn't surprised.

"You know what," Emma said with a heavy sigh, "never mind, Ma."

Minnie, it seemed, had already moved on. "Your father and uncle will be here soon for dinner. You did bring along a nanny or something for the boy, right?"

"No."

"No?"

It was almost laughable how shocked her mother sounded.

Emma wished she cared.

"No," Emma repeated, walking on past her mother to go find Calisto and her son. "See, I'm trying this thing that you never did, Ma. It's called actually *raising* and loving my child."

"We loved you."

Emma scoffed. "Not nearly enough, and only when it was convenient for you."

That, Minnie didn't deny.

She couldn't.

"Calisto, take a walk with me, and we'll talk." Maximo smiled across the table. "Like all good Dons should do, yes?"

Calisto looked to Emma, a silent question in his eyes. *Is that okay?*

Emma nodded, and Calisto passed their napping son over into her waiting arms. It wasn't long before Calisto and Maximo had disappeared from the dining room, leaving Emma alone with her father.

Minnie had long excused herself to bed.

Thank God.

"You're looking quite well, Emma," her father said.

Emma smiled at George. "Thank you, Daddy."

"And the little one, he seems happy. Healthy, too."

She held Cross a bit tighter. "He is."

"I wondered how you would fare as a mother," George admitted. "A wife, I had no worries. You were raised for that position. A mother, however, is a different story."

"And why is that?"

George sipped from his whiskey, shrugging. "It's hard to connect and care for children that are, in a way, forced upon you. I told you to marry Affonso, but he was the one who demanded the offspring. I don't think it's the same thing."

She had news for her father.

"It's exactly the same thing. Except I do love my son. Entirely. He was simply born. He didn't ask to be."

"Fair enough," her father conceded. "Although, you've done quite well for yourself, haven't you? Regardless of Affonso's doings, you have still managed to do well *and* keep your position. I'm quite proud of you for that."

Emma's brow furrowed. "Pardon?"

George smirked. "Your *new* husband, Emma. It's an embarrassing shame that Affonso did what he did; up and leaving, and then sending divorce papers after he was gone, never to show his face again. And yet, here you are, married again to another boss, your position and respect intact. Shame about the divorce, of course, but I believe that given everything else you managed to accomplish, we can overlook that misstep."

Emma was struck silent, stuck between being unsure that she had heard her father properly, and being extremely offended *because* she had heard him just fine. She knew that the story he repeated to her was the one that had been offered to the public; it was widely accepted and believed. It was the same as how people believed that Cross was actually Affonso's son, and not Calisto's, but that didn't mean Emma had to like it. Sure, it was the safe story and route to go to protect their lives and reputations, but it was still fucking offensive.

She loved Calisto.

He loved her.

She wished there didn't have to be a whole story,

as fake as it was, to go along with it.

"I …" Emma's words failed her for a minute. "I'm happy that at least one thing I have done in my life has made you proud, Daddy."

She meant none of it.

George looked as pleased as ever.

Emma just felt sick. "Excuse me for a second."

"I can hold the boy, if—"

"No, it's fine," Emma rushed to say.

Like *fuck* would she ever be handing her son over to her mother or father. Never. Once upon a time, she would have given anything to see her parents soften toward her or her children. Now, she just couldn't find it in her heart to give a shit.

Cross had a mother and a father who loved him, who would never do to him what had been done to them, by the people who should have loved them. He had a whole army of people—Donati people—to look after him, and walk him through life. Calisto was making sure of that. Emma, too.

Cross didn't need these people.

Neither did Emma.

Not anymore.

She was gone from the dining room without bothering to say goodbye to her father. Soon, she found Calisto sitting in the upstairs office with her uncle. Maximo looked irritated to have his conversation intruded upon. Calisto only looked concerned to see Emma standing in the doorway.

"Not now, Emma," Maximo said. "We're almost do—"

Calisto held up a hand, stopping Maximo from saying more. He only looked to Emma, his wife, the one person he cared about the most alongside his son. It was something that Maximo couldn't possibly understand, Emma thought.

"Emmy?" Calisto asked.

"I'm ready, Cal."

He didn't ask what she meant.

He didn't have to.

Their jet was in the air in less than two hours.

DONATI
EXTENDED FILE

4.
DONATI
EXTENDED FILE #1

Thin Lies – Chapter Twenty

Author's Note: ***Thin Lies*** **was certainly a slow burn for the readers, as far as romantic (read: sex) scenes goes. Even the first scene that dealt with something sexual between the main characters was not full on sex; that came shortly after. But the first full scene was cut short, as while the readers waited a long time for it, the scene was simply *too* long. Even for one of my scenes. This is what had to be cut from that scene; the morning after.**

Emma let the steaming hot water of the shower work out the kinks in her sore, tired muscles. She focused on massaging the shampoo into her hair, and not the sinfully sexy man she had left sleeping in her bed.

Calisto.

Even in the safe privacy of her mind, she breathed his name like a prayer.

That was bad.

So. Fucking. Bad.

It was not like Emma to wake up early, especially not before ten. It also wasn't like her to share a bed with a man, either. It only took the hard warmth of Calisto's body pushing against Emma's naked back, and she had suddenly been wide awake.

Wet and sore between her thighs.

Hot all over.

Horny as fuck.

Awake.

Same difference.

Emma scrubbed her hands through her hair with a bit more force than was necessary, hoping that would get her mind away from those thoughts. The distraction did the trick, as the sting in her scalp helped her to ignore the ache between her thighs.

What did you do?

Emma ignored her inner voice, knowing damn well that it would do her no good to feed into the self-deprecating thoughts. At least, not right now.

She had just finished rinsing the soap from her hair when she heard the shower door slide open. Her vision was blurry from the spray of water, but even still, she saw the unmistakeable shape of Calisto sliding inside the shower.

Naked.

Of course.

Calisto reached for the soap on the corner shelf behind Emma. "You don't mind, do you? Sharing, I mean."

Emma shook her head.

What was she going to say?

Yes, it bothered her?

No, he should wait?

After last night?

And she wouldn't even mean those things if she did say them.

"Flight lifts off in four hours," Calisto said.

Emma barely heard him.

Soap. Muscles. Hot water. Gorgeous body.

"What?" she managed to ask.

How could he look that good just taking a fucking shower?

Emma was clearly punishing herself now. The rest of her life was sure to be fun.

"The flight," Calisto said. "In four hours."

Emma swallowed the heat in her voice, saying, "Okay, great."

"You okay?"

"Hmm?"

Seriously, there wasn't a mark on Calisto's body. No tattoos. No blemishes. No scars that stood out. He was incredibly fit, from the definition of his chest, to the hard chiseled V of his groin. Emma was sure she would have noticed all of those details the night before, had it all not happened so fast. She had been so caught up that she hadn't properly admired Calisto.

What a shame.

And a waste.

Emma's gaze once again took inventory of the beautiful man, starting from the top, and working her way down. Only this time, she found his cock was jutting out—hard, long, and proud.

Jesus.

"You're going to give me a complex, *donna*."

Emma's gaze snapped up to meet Calisto's in an instant, heat filling her cheeks. "I'm sorry?"

"You heard what I said."

Why was he smirking?

Goddamn him.

"I just—"

"What?" Calisto asked.

"I didn't stop to admire last night, that's all. You're not giving me much of a choice right now."

"Oh?"

"That's my story, Cal." She eye-fucked him again, unashamed. "Do you spend a lot of time in the gym, or …?"

"I box, occasionally."

"Huh."

"And I run when I can."

"That would help."

"But it's mostly good genes," he added with a hint of bitter sarcasm.

"I bet."

Emma decided then and there that she needed to get the hell out of that shower, and far away from this man. Just to take a breather, for some space, at the very least. Last night had been enough. As it was, their *just once* had turned into twice.

She had already fucked up.

She indulged when she knew better.

Emma didn't even get to make it fully past Calisto before he had grabbed hold of her wrist and pulled her back. Her mouth opened with a question—maybe even a rebuttal—only to be quieted by his kiss.

And fuck, could the man kiss.

She was made weak by his mouth alone. Struck silent in his demand and force. The slow strokes of his tongue exploring her mouth was a sinful reminder of what he felt like eating her pussy.

Emma was gone again.

Just like that.

"Fucking hell, your mouth," Calisto grunted against her lips. "Drives me insane, Emmy."

The hard length of his erection pressed against her stomach, heavy and hot and *fuck*.

He didn't ask for permission as he backed her into the tiled wall, out of the reach of the shower's spray. But then again, he didn't really have to ask. Emma's lust and desire was screaming far louder than the rational side of her brain.

It sounded a lot like it was begging for *Calisto*, and *yes*, and *more*.

That could have also been her saying those things out loud, but Emma wasn't really sure.

She was too far gone.

And she didn't even care.

Calisto didn't even have to ask for her legs to widen, and she barely got in a breath as he lifted her to the wall. His hand slid between their bodies, she felt the nudge of his cock against her folds, and that was it.

All her air left.

All her thoughts disappeared.

One flex of his hips forward, and Emma was fucking *full* again. Blissfully full and aching. She was damn wet, too, and that only aided in sensation of his cock dragging along her inner walls and nerves with his next thrust.

"Fuck," she mumbled.

Calisto hummed, deep and satisfied. "Yeah."

"*Fuck.*"

The second one of her curses seemed to come out more like a whine. She couldn't help it.

A tenderness settled in her pussy, a sweet, yet bitter aftereffect of the night before. Yet, she didn't mind. It certainly didn't make her want to stop, or even to ask him to slow.

If anything, it made it better.

She felt *more*.

She felt him deeper.

He was watching her, too, she found. Dark eyes, parted lips, and sex on his tongue. He watched her.

It was such a shame, she thought.

How good they could have been outside of this.

How good they had been.

How good it could have been.

How good *this* was.

Life certainly wasn't fair for them.

Funny, though, how she didn't care about life when Calisto was fucking her.

DONATI
UNSEEN FILES

Author's Note: Unseen files are typically events that take place after the last chapter of the final book, *Thin Lives*, but before the actual Epilogue, as that was twenty years into the future. These are not deleted scenes, but rather, events that readers expressed interest in seeing, and as such, were written exclusively for the *Collection*, and *Behind the Bloodlines*.

—Kris

5.
DONATI
UNSEEN FILES #1

The Donati Prince

Calisto watched as Cross's dark curls bobbed up and down, in and out of his father's sight from the other side of the desk. The two year old toddler had strewn cars, trucks, and trains from one end of his father's office, to the other. Calisto should have been focusing on the documents that he had yet to go through on a business he was considering buying, but Cross's fun and noise was keeping him distracted.

Not that Calisto minded, really.

His son—although his nephew to the outside world—was his pride.

His very greatest pride.

And the boy was only two.

Calisto could only imagine what Cross would be like as a young man. So for now, he did his very best to keep Cross close, to give him time, affection, and love that he would remember long after his younger years were forgotten.

Time, love, and affection that was so unlike what he had been given growing up under the man who had meant to be his father-figure. As a boy, he remembered being adored by Affonso, sure, but now it was tainted with all the lies, secrets, and manipulations to go along with it.

Calisto didn't want that to be him and Cross in twenty or so years, when his boy looked back on his life with the man who raised him.

"Vroom, vroom, vroom, vroom!" Cross screeched, chasing a self-propelled car with one he was pushing. Then, the toys, and the toddler, crashed into the far wall. "*Boom.*"

Cross had mumbled the word at the same time he crashed into the wall. Calisto had all he could do to hold back the laughter.

He briefly wondered if Cross had hurt himself, but it didn't last long. Cross groaned before rolling over, grabbing his cars, and beginning the game all over again. Perfectly safe, entirely unscathed.

As usual.

Calisto tried not to coddle his son too much. It was a sad fact of their life, but when his boy was older, no one would be watching Cross's back, or standing him up on his own two feet when he crashed and burned. Cross, like Calisto, would have to eventually learn over time to do those things on his own.

So as much as he struggled and wavered, and as much as it sometimes killed him to see the tears well in Cross's eyes every time he fell, missed a step, or if he got a little out of hand when he played, Calisto stayed back.

As long as there was no blood, no broken bones, and no visible bumps, Calisto let Cross learn to self-soothe and self-care.

It was not a *boys will be boys* sort of mentality, either.

For Calisto, it was more of a *this boy needs to learn that he can handle things, and fix them, on his own.*

Sometimes, Calisto failed, too.

Sometimes, he simply reacted to the sudden cries of his two year old son, only to find the boy had jammed his finger trying to sneak a cookie. Or even when Cross was pissed because his mother's dog had stolen his toy.

But he thought, even in those moments, Cross knew exactly what he was doing. He would look to Calisto with the knowing smile and genuine joy only a toddler could have. He imagined in those moments, that Cross was thinking, *See, Papa, I knew you would come.*

Sometimes, it only took the right cry.

Sometimes, a louder than normal bang.

Sometimes, it was just Cross's babyish, boyish giggles and his voice calling, "Da!"

Calisto would run.

Cross would be waiting.

"Da," came the child-like voice at his feet.

Calisto broke from his daze to see Cross sitting on the floor, holding up a car for him to take. It was red, with a bright yellow racing stripe.

Cross's favorite car.

"Da," Cross said again, offering the toy still.

"Play, Da."

Calisto thought to correct his son about calling him his father, as he usually did when others were around. Though he had legally adopted Cross, everyone else knew him as the boy's uncle, and it was safer that way. He often corrected the boy to say *Zio*, and not the Da or Papa that Cross preferred to use.

That killed Calisto, too.

But no one was there, no one who would care, anyway.

Calisto corrected nothing.

He preferred Da or Papa, too.

"Play?" Cross asked again. "Please, Da."

He had work to do.

It was well past seven, and his son's bedtime.

Calisto didn't care.

He got down on the office floor, and played with his son until Cross crawled into his lap, his car in hand, and fell asleep.

These were the moments that he hoped Cross remembered the most.

These ones right here.

Calisto didn't realize how long he had stayed like

that, holding his sleeping son on the floor, until his wife arrived home and was standing in the office doorway. Emma didn't go out with friends very often, so when she did, Calisto said nothing about it, simply let her go and have her bit of fun.

She was the love of his life.

The very best mother, too.

"Why didn't you put him to bed?" she asked.

Calisto shrugged. "Because."

"Because why?"

"Because someday, he'll be older, Emmy. He won't want to play on the floor, and he certainly won't want to play with me."

Because that's what happened when little princes grew up to be kings.

6.
DONATI
UNSEEN FILES #2

Principessa

"But, Emma—"

"Cal, we've been over this a hundred times already. It's too risky."

He knew that.

She was right.

"We know, though. And Cross was perfectly fine at thirty-two weeks, just a bit small."

"Cal, he spent over a week in the hospital, had jaundice, difficulty latching, and just the fact that he was even *that* healthy considering his gestational age at birth was nothing more than fucking luck."

Calisto sighed, rubbing a hand down his jaw to ease the tension settling there. It didn't really help. He fucking hated fighting with his wife, even if this wasn't technically them fighting, per say. But he wanted this one thing for them, and him, so badly, that he was willing to risk it turning into a fight just on the off chance his desires would be heard. A simple "no" was not going to be good enough for this.

"Emma, just think about it."

His wife turned on her heel in the walk-in closet, stopping Calisto from following her further. Anger and hurt blazed in her eyes. "Do you really think that I haven't stopped to *consider* something like that?"

"Well—"

"Do you think I'm that callous?"

"I never said that," Calisto rushed to say. "And I never would, Emmy."

"Good," Emma replied sharply. "But in case you might have forgotten, I *can't* not think about it, Cal. It's my body; my babies lost. One on a kitchen floor, and one in a graveyard. How dare anyone, but especially you, even suggest that I don't, or can't, think of having another child, when I've already lost two? I think about another—and them—all the fucking time!"

Calisto felt properly chastised for speaking without, at the very least, considering his wife's feelings. "I'm sorry, Emma. That wasn't what I meant to say, or how I meant for it to sound, and I'm sorry if I made you feel that way."

Emma glanced away, but not before Calisto saw the tears gathering in her eyes. "I know you want another baby."

"Not to the detriment of us, though."

She nodded. "I thought Cross was going to be enough."

Calisto quickly crossed the space between him and his wife, taking Emma into his embrace and holding her tight. He carefully wiped the silent tears from her cheeks, and then kissed her softly.

"He is enough. He has always been enough, Emma."

"But he's not yours, too, right?" she asked quietly. "Not to everyone else, and I know how much that kills you inside. They look at him and think he's Affonso's boy, not yours. I see it in your eyes every time you have to correct him to call you uncle in front of others. Or worse, when someone else calls you his uncle to him. You raise him, you love him, and yet, he can't fully be yours to them, even if he really is."

Calisto frowned. He hated that his one thing— his one cause of sadness—was so clear and on display for his wife. She didn't need to be burdened with these sorts of things. It was his issue, something he had done and it was his sole choice to continue. Even if it hurt him, and it did, it was in the best interests of his wife and son. Emma knew this, of course, but that didn't make it easier on either of them.

"He is enough," Calisto repeated.

"But?"

"There doesn't have to be a 'but' at all, Emma."

"But is there?"

Sort of.

Probably not what she thought, though.

"I see you too, you know," Calisto murmured into Emma's hair. "But especially when you think that I don't. When you get invited to a baby shower. Or when you see babies at the park. When someone asks about a sibling for Cross. I see, too, Emma."

She sighed. "I think about it all the time, but I

think about a kitchen floor and a tiny casket, too."

Yeah, he knew that now.

Calisto wasn't so selfish of a man, or so full of foolish pride, that he would hurt his wife in an effort to fill their house with more children.

"As long as we're happy like we are," Calisto said, "then nothing else matters. Right?"

"But are we?"

That was the million dollar question.

"I don't know, Emmy. You tell me. I'm leaving this up to you, now. I won't say another thing about it until you do."

"Cal ... Calisto!"

The sheer desperation in Emma's scream sent Calisto flying from his office. Three and a half year old Cross stumbled after his father, likely confused.

"Cal!"

He wasn't quite sure what to expect as he took

the stairs three at a time to the second level. Emma had been napping, as she needed her rest. Especially now, considering her state.

Rest.

Relaxation.

No stress.

Those were the doctor's orders. They had been the doctor's orders from the day, fifteen weeks earlier, when they found out they were expecting their second child, and that his wife had already been a month along at that point.

"Cal!"

Each time that Emma shrieked for him, her voice became impossibly higher. More terrified. Heartbroken, even.

He found his nineteen-week pregnant wife on the middle of their bed, straddling a small streak of red that stained the white sheets. Emma looked to him, horrified. That expression she wore was so sadly familiar; he had seen it on her before, remembered all too vividly her pain and terror as he opened a public bathroom stall in a restaurant only to find her miscarrying her unborn child.

Calisto knew what Emma was going to say before she even said it. He still let her.

"It's happening again," Emma rasped.

He was stunned, frozen to the spot, and so fucking useless in that moment. Things were supposed to be good with the pregnancy, even the doctors thought so. Twice weekly appointments to monitor the baby and Emma's cervix had given them a sense of security that everything would be just fine.

It was a false sense, clearly.

It took the smallest gasp from Cross to finally break Calisto from his stupor. The boy pushed past his father and moved further into the bedroom, pointing his finger right at his mother with wide eyes.

"Oh, noes," Cross said loudly, "Ma's got a bleeds!"

Emma's tears flowed harder, which only spurred tiny Cross into his own round of cries. Likely at the confusion of what was happening around him. His small world was not usually so chaotic and unsure.

Calisto said nothing as he scooped his now wailing son into his arms, grabbed the cordless phone on the nightstand, and made a call. Twenty-four-seven, he had someone watching the house, or very close by. Less than three minutes later, Calisto passed his son off to the enforcer that rushed inside the house.

By that time, Emma had managed to get out of the bed and make her way to the stairs. Calisto met her there, and carried his wife to their own car. He didn't care to call emergency services and wait for an ambulance.

He would *always* make it there faster.

"Oh, I'm sorry," the ultrasound technician said, giving a squirming Cross an annoyed look. "Our policy is not to allow young children, even siblings, into the room."

Calisto glared, refusing to let go of his son who wanted down on the floor. "You're fucking kidding me, right?"

"Uh, well, no."

Emma glanced up at Calisto from her wheelchair, a staple in her daily life since being admitted to the hospital two weeks prior. "It's ... okay."

"See," the tech said, far too chipper for Calisto's liking. "You can handle the little one. She will be fine to go in alone."

No.

Hell no.

It was most certainly *not* fine.

Calisto barked out a laugh before he could check the impulse. "No, I'll be going in, and so will our son."

The tech put her hands on her hips. "Policy says—"

"Fuck your policy," Calisto snapped. "I don't know if you've bothered to give more than a passing glance at my wife, or if she's just another appointment for you, but take a moment to do that."

The woman did, and Calisto knew exactly what she was seeing. A tired, worried Emma who looked small in her chair, and really just needed to get this whole day over with.

"She's in a hospital gown, in a hospital-issued

wheelchair," Calisto said before the woman could speak again. "Because right now, and for the unforeseeable future, this hospital is where she fucking lives. Her pregnancy is so high risk, that for the moment, the doctors can't afford for her to be outside of this place. Now, I know you probably haven't opened her file yet to know what you need to check for on the ultrasound, so you don't really know any of these things, but let me fill you in really quick."

Calisto smiled, but it was cold. "The only thing that is keeping my child inside my wife's body right now is a hope, a prayer, and a goddamn fucking stitch. A stitch that may or may not be infected, but we have to wait until the specialist finishes his appointments for the day before we can get a start on those tests. Now, we had the option of having a portable ultrasound machine brought up into my wife's room today, but given she hasn't seen the outside of it since she had the stitch put in, the nurses and I thought that she might like a bit of a break by taking a trip down here."

"Mr.—"

"Shut up and listen," Calisto interjected sharply.

"Cal," Emma murmured.

He ignored his wife.

She was not the type to cause a fuss, while he most certainly would.

"This is literally a day-by-day thing for us right now. One day, to the next, and then to the next again. That's how we've been told to treat this pregnancy, at least with the hopes we will make it to a safe threshold so that our child is *viable*."

Calisto ran his hand through Cross's mop of black curls. "So today is one of the only days that our son has been able to come in and see his mother this week. And we told him that he would also be able to see his baby brother or sister today on the screen. Do you understand what that means?"

"No," the tech admitted.

"It means: Fuck. Your. Policy."

Cross got to see his sibling.

Calisto and Emma learned they were having a beautiful little girl.

A princess.

A Donati *principessa*.

"Papa?"

Calisto's eyes cracked open to see the darkness of his bedroom staring back at him. He was acutely aware of how empty his bed was without his wife sleeping beside him. It felt cold and uninviting, but he didn't have much of a choice.

His bed would continue to be a cold and empty place until Emma was back at home. He spent as much time at the hospital as he possibly could, but with their newly turned four year old, his position in *la famiglia*, and life in general, his time had to be split between the hospital, home, and the business.

Speaking of Cross …

"Papa, can I sleeps with you?"

Calisto blinked awake further, his gaze focusing on Cross standing just a foot away from his side of the bed. In one hand, Cross clutched his favorite blanket. His other hand was stuck in his mouth. Or rather, his thumb was.

"Cross," Calisto mumbled.

The boy's thumb slipped from his mouth with a wet, loud pop. "Yeah, Papa?"

Calisto sighed, trying to decide which issue to deal with first where his son was concerned. The fact Cross was out of his bed, or sucking his thumb. The 'Papa' thing was a whole other matter. Cross called Calisto his father whether he was corrected on it or not, however, he had learned not to do it in front of others.

"Why are you out of bed, buddy?" Calisto asked.

"Wanna see Ma," Cross said simply.

"Ma is at the hospital to—"

"Keep baby Camilla safe. I *knows*, Papa."

Calisto had to hold back his chuckle at all the attitude his four year old had managed to stuff into that one sentence. He rubbed a hand over his jaw, noting he needed a good shave, and wondered what fucking time it even was.

"Will baby Camilla come home when Ma comes, too?" Cross asked.

Damn.

For such a little boy, Cross sure asked some

difficult as fuck questions.

"Probably not," Calisto said.

"Why?"

Because their daughter—who they had decided to name early simply to give themselves hope and Cross something tangible as to why his mother was away—would likely be born far too early, even with all the help she had keeping her safe.

How could Calisto possibly explain that to Cross?

"Because baby Camilla might still need more time to let the doctors help make her better," Calisto settled on saying.

"Oh. Okay."

That was that, it seemed.

Cross stuck his thumb back in his mouth. Calisto checked the urge to tell the boy to stop, but only because Cross used thumb-sucking as a comfort during difficult moments. He rarely sucked his thumb at all, actually. That behavior only showed itself if he was extremely stressed out, or upset by something. Calisto figured Cross's thumb-sucking, added onto his questions, and his late night visit to his father's bed was a damn good indication about just how troubled the boy was with what was happening in his life.

"Wanna see Ma," Cross mumbled around his thumb.

Calisto frowned. "Me, too, buddy. Me, too."

But visiting time was hours away yet.

So was morning, according to the clock.

Calisto pulled his son up into the bed, turned on his phone to gallery images of their family, handed it over to Cross to swipe through, and hoped it did something for the boy. It was all he could do, really. At least for a few more hours. Cross found a picture he liked, tucked the phone into the blankets between him and his father, and promptly fell asleep.

Calisto didn't shut his eyes again.

He couldn't when he knew that life was waiting to wake him up.

Twenty-nine weeks.

That was how long Emma's body had allowed the stitch to stay in place before infection forced an early morning C-section.

Camilla Emma Donati.

Named for the two strongest women that Calisto had ever known.

Cross had been so distraught when Calisto told him that his sister had been born, but he would not be allowed inside the NICU to see her.

Emma cried the day her release papers had been signed, yet she needed to leave her daughter behind for God knew how long.

And Calisto?

He soothed his son and held Cross up for hours against the NICU windows so he could peer inside and see baby Camilla. He comforted his wife when she needed him to, and when she would allow him to help.

He never admitted how guilty he felt to see his daughter struggle for a life that *he* had been the one to beg for her to have. He never said a word about how it killed him to feel her weightlessness or hear her soundless sobs when she tried to cry. Every wire, tube, and lead on her tiny body was like a knife slicing through his skin.

The first time he had been able to hold her, he was *terrified*. She was dwarfed by his size, but all her little warmth bled into his, and that helped. He wished that she didn't have to fight for breath, or the ability to eat. He hated seeing her eyes taped shut for those first weeks, when he only wanted to have her look at him, her father. He wanted her home, in his arms or her mother's, but certainly *not* in an incubator for well over a month.

Nothing had been harder than leaving the NICU day after day, knowing all their daughter had for comfort were the nurses to hold her, soothe her, or rock and feed her when she needed it. And while those nurses were some of the most amazing people Calisto had ever come in contact with, he also knew they had another half of a dozen babies in the same, if not worse, position than Camilla on any given day.

Fifty-fifty. Those were the chances given to each and every premature newborn born while Camilla waited out her stay in the NICU. Camilla landed on the good side of the fifty-fifty coin. Too many other babies did not.

But Camilla grew.

She became stronger.

She ate.

She made noise.

She gained weight, although slowly.

And the day they brought her home, still preemie small, but alive?

He was even *more* terrified.

But he loved her still.

God, how loved Camilla was.

His little Donati *principessa*.

All the hell and fear and the pain was worth it, then.

And Calisto couldn't regret or feel any guilt for that.

7.
DONATI
UNSEEN FILES #3

Cross + Catherine

Calisto shifted on the hard chair, and checked the incoming text on his phone.

So?

That was all the message read.

Same as the last time you checked, Calisto texted back to his wife. He managed to hold back from adding that instead of texting him every five damn seconds, she could have just come with him when the phone call came in.

Not that the phone call had given them very much to go on. Cross, in his senior year of high school, had managed to get himself in some kind of trouble that involved two other students. He would be suspended for seven days, would be benched for several upcoming games with his teams, and would need to be picked up and removed from the school property by a parent immediately.

Apparently, Cross wasn't even allowed to drive his new Range Rover home. The school asked Calisto to take care of that, too, which he had. He had given the spare set of keys to one of his enforcers, then directed the man to park the Rover in the Donati garage until further notice. Depending on how this meeting went would determine when, or if at all, Cross would get his keys back.

And of course, it was also determined by what his son had to say about it all. Calisto had come to learn with the school and Cross that details were sometimes left out.

It wasn't often that the nearly eighteen year old Cross actually found himself in trouble at school. God knew the kid had more than enough trouble to find all around him outside of school. Cross wasn't on a short leash, and Calisto didn't force a lot of rules onto his son.

It would do him no good.

He learned that long ago.

As it was, Calisto was just grateful that Cross had half of a mind to at least *finish* high school. Especially considering his son was far more interested in the family business, and his likeness of guns instead of furthering his education.

Calisto didn't say a negative word to his boy either way, though he did demand that Cross finish school. Cross had to make his own choices regarding the family business and the mafia on his own, so then later in life, he didn't find regret looking back.

Outside of school, Calisto put few restraints on Cross.

At school, however, he did ask his son for a few things regarding the private establishment for Cross's, and their family's, privacy, safety, and to keep his kid out of fucking juvenile detention.

Obvious, simple things.

No weapons at school; guns, knives, or otherwise.

No talking about family business, even to other students or friends that shared their lifestyle, as the Donati *principe* was just *one* child of a mafia boss attending the private school.

No drugs, using especially, but more importantly, selling. Calisto wasn't stupid, and he didn't stick his head in the damn sand like too many parents did. Cross dabbled in things from time to time, usually in his off seasons from sports to avoid being removed from the teams, and almost always at parties or something of that nature. His son was honest about it all, so Calisto chose to trust that Cross would keep his private business clean enough to stay out of trouble.

No racing his vehicles, causing a problem, and so forth.

Finally, no sex on school property. Something had happened once, apparently in a vehicle, and Cross and another student had been accused of ... things. There certainly hadn't been enough proof for the school to do anything, except make a fuss, a phone call, and a threat to suspend Cross, but Cross had not denied the event when asked by his father, either. In fact, his son had smirked, shrugged, and freely offered the information that Calisto was not to worry, that Cross was always *safe*.

The other student involved in that particular

incident?

Catherine Cecelia Marcello.

The daughter of the long reigning, most powerful Italian Cosa Nostra boss in New York, Dante Marcello.

Which, at the time, just made shit so much more complicated, awkward, and difficult.

That had been several months ago, nearing the end of Cross's eleventh year, and Catherine's tenth. As far as Calisto knew, the two teenagers had gone on yet another break in their long on again, off again relationship.

Now that it was just the first month of Cross's final year, Calisto thought whatever trouble his son was in might not bode well for rest of his senior year. Calisto hadn't even stopped to consider for a second that the trouble this time might somehow relate to Catherine Marcello again, though.

Or, that was what Calisto assumed.

Until he shifted in the uncomfortable chair again, glanced up, and watched Dante Marcello walk in through the office doors. In that moment, Calisto had the strangest urge to do two things. One, smack himself in the face. And two, throttle the fuck out of his son.

Cross, what did you do now?

"Afternoon, Calisto," Dante said, looking entirely unpleased as he took a seat.

"Afternoon, Dante."

The two bosses sat in silence for several minutes before Dante spoke up again.

"For the tuition we pay into this place, one might think they would invest in more comfortable chairs."

"I think it's a purposeful move. You can sit for a while in your own discomfort and think about what you've done." Calisto chuckled. "Or what your kid has fucked up on."

Dante scowled. "Jesus, that brings back way too many memories of my own school years."

"Spent a lot of time in the principal's office, did you?" Calisto asked, amused.

"Did you?"

"A bit."

Dante smiled. "My poor parents had three boys attending high school all at the same time at one point. We raised hell. Actually nearly got expelled one by one within a single semester. Antony had to run in to the school every single day to deal with something we had done for a spell."

"I'm suddenly feeling grateful that Cross is mostly ..."

"Sneaky?" Dante offered.

"You know, that's probably as good a word as any."

"All boys of made men are, or they learn to be, I suppose."

Calisto had to agree. "What did Antony do to make you three chill out in the end?"

"Nothing. My mother was the one, actually."

"Oh?"

"She cried," Dante admitted. "She was so angry and disappointed that she just cried. That was mostly the end of that."

"I can understand that."

"But ... you would have to understand my father, too. We made Cecelia Marcello cry, and no man has been known to survive that once Antony finds out."

"Shit."

"The fear of God was named Antony in our home." Dante grinned. "But only when it came to our mother and Cosa Nostra. Other than those times, he was just dad to us, but that switch, man, that fucking switch of his could flip when we walked those lines. We knew."

Dante shrugged, adding, "Otherwise, he just let us boys …"

"Do your own thing."

"Yes."

Like Calisto was trying to do with Cross.

"Smart man," Calisto noted.

"He certainly put us on a path to follow. It's done each of us brothers well in our own ways. None of us necessarily walked the path the same way, but we all made it to the end alive. I suppose in that, Antony succeeded the most, considering."

"True." Calisto glanced at the closed office doors. "Did they say anything—"

"Not a damn word," Dante interjected gruffly.

"Great."

Dante passed Calisto a cold look. "And as long as it isn't another incident like the car one from last year, your son will live to see another day."

Ah.

There it was.

"You know, it does take two. You have children, and a wife, so you're aware how sex works between people. And, you *were* a teenage boy once. Tell me that you don't understand those complexities, Dante."

"I know I never got caught between the thighs of a boss's daughter in the back seat of the Lexus her father just bought her for her birthday."

Well, then.

"Point taken," Calisto muttered. "To be fair, I do think my son cares quite a bit for Catherine in the grand scheme of things."

"Yes, love. She told me that once—he *loved* her, she loves him. In ten years, they will barely remember one another's names."

Calisto wasn't so sure on that. If only because Cross kept returning to Catherine even if it got him in ten shades of shit for doing so. Calisto opted not to point that out to Dante, considering the man's already temperamental mood.

"Would it be such a bad thing," Calisto dared to

say, "if in ten years, what you think might happen, is actually the furthest thing from reality?"

The office door opened, exposing a waiting, displeased principal.

Wonder-fucking-ful.

"As long as he loves my daughter, and not some puppy nonsense like he has now," Dante said quietly, "but truly loves her, then no, it would not be such a bad thing, as you say. I have no intention of doing to my children what was done to too many others, and choosing their futures, their spouses, or making demands of their lives. But with that said, Cross has one hell of a long way to go, Calisto."

"Mr. Donati, Mr. Marcello, thanks for coming in so quickly. Follow me, your children are waiting inside, although Catherine can return to classes tomorrow, but Cross—"

"Yeah, a week," Calisto interrupted. "I know."

Although, Catherine's lighter punishment, if that's even what it was, boded well for the situation. Surely she would have also gotten a similar suspension to Cross's punishment had they been …

"The other boy involved has been taken to the

hospital by his mother," the principal said. "We're waiting to hear if they're planning to press any charges or not."

"Back up," Calisto said. "Who did what now?"

The woman sighed. "Well, we don't really know. Seems neither your son, your daughter, *nor* the boy with the broken nose and black eyes wants to talk. We suspect it was a tiff between the boys over Catherine, as she's been seen with the one who was injured lately, but we're also aware of her *old* relationship with Cross."

Dante stiffened. "Did you ask my daughter that?"

"Of course."

"And?"

"And your daughter lives up to her surname, Mr. Marcello. Nothing to hear, nothing to say."

Calisto swore he saw Dante smirk out of the corner of his eye.

The bastard.

"So if nothing is known, then why is my son being suspended?" Calisto demanded.

"Because, one boy has a broken face, and *your*

son is the one with the busted up knuckles and a smartass answer for everything."

Of course he was.

Dammit, Cross.

"Please, collect your children. Write-ups have been filed. I would like to keep this from happening again, if at all possible."

Both Dante and Calisto agreed. But, Calisto seriously doubted that neither he, nor his counterpart, could honestly make that promise given the teenagers actions thus far together.

Calisto found his son sitting opposite to Catherine Marcello in the principal's office. The pretty, young girl stood at the sight of her father, and headed in Dante's direction without a word.

But not before Calisto caught the small smile she shot to Cross before leaving.

That left Calisto alone with his son.

"Well," Calisto started, "what do you have to say?"

Cross stood to his full height, tossing his backpack over his shoulder. At almost eighteen, Cross already stood slightly taller than his father at six foot, three inches.

"Nothing to say," Cross muttered.

"Try again, Cross."

Cross shrugged. "It's like this, I'm always going to have Catherine's back, regardless. If she needs something, she knows where to come. No questions asked. She came, she asked for help, I dealt with it."

Dealt with what?

Calisto shot a look over his shoulder, noting the door had been closed, allowing them privacy. "I thought you two weren't together now?"

"We don't have to be, all right?"

Calisto wondered if maybe Dante didn't see what he saw in Cross every time his son talked about Catherine. Sure, Cross was young. He did stupid shit sometimes.

But he loved that girl.

Calisto knew he did.

"And what did she ask for this time?" Calisto asked.

"Doesn't matter." Cross cocked a brow. "I handled it."

"Yes, by breaking someone's face and getting

suspended. So for one fucking second here, you can indulge me, Cross. I don't ask very much of you. Explain it to me."

Cross frowned. "I said I wouldn't tell, Papa."

"Neither will I. Start talking."

"The guy she's been dating ... I guess he took some pictures on his phone last weekend after a party when she went home with him, or whatever. He's been using them to try and get her to do shit."

Calisto let out a hard exhale.

That was not what he had been expecting to hear.

"Oh," he said dumbly.

"Catherine's not like some of these girls, all right? She doesn't do that kind of shit, take pictures and send them out, or whatever. She just doesn't, she's too smart for fucking shit like that. He didn't ask, or so she says, and had the pictures to show anybody whenever he wanted to."

"So you took care of it."

Cross nodded. "I guess."

"And the pictures?"

Cross pulled a phone from his jacket pocket.

"Android, no cloud, no backup. All messages sent have been checked. All the pictures have been deleted."

"Good," Calisto said.

"I'm going to drop it off to Tommy and get him to double check before I destroy the fucking thing, but I'm sure it's good."

"All right. And what about you and Catherine?"

"What about us?"

"Are you together now, or …?" Calisto let his question hang open for his son to answer or not.

Cross just stared at his father, bored. "I told you, we *don't have to be*. I've always got her back, no matter what."

Yeah.

Ten years for Cross and Catherine.

Calisto would bet his fucking life and fortune on those ten years.

Maybe even less.

"Your Rover keys will be on my desk when you get home; you are free to do whatever the hell you want on your suspension, Cross," Calisto said. "But try to stay out of more trouble, please, and for your mother's sake, tone down on the suspensions and fighting. She frets, and then I have to listen to it day in and day out, I swear it's going to give me a fucking stroke."

There was absolutely no way in hell that Calisto was going to punish his son for this. The school could do whatever they wanted, but Calisto was of a different mindset. He also understood why Cross, Catherine, and the boy who got a well-deserved ass-kicking didn't speak up. The foolish kid didn't want to get in trouble for what he had done, and Catherine probably didn't want her parents finding out the truth.

Cross, on the other hand, kept his mouth shut for Catherine.

Ten years.

"I'm serious, Cross," Calisto said as he walked out of the office with his son. "Tone it down a little."

"Will do."

"Perfect."

That was the end of that.

8.
DONATI
UNSEEN FILES #4

Dreaded Moments

There were moments in every mother's life that she waited for, in a constant state of dread, even when she was happy. A midnight phone call, an accident at home, or … something. It all revolved around her children, and an event that might take them before their time.

The circle of life should be that children buried their parents, not the other way around. But sometimes, life was cruel, and what should be ended up much different than what anyone wanted or planned for.

It had always been a fear of Emma's that she might be the mother to get that late-night phone call, or find an officer standing at her front door.

Her fear had only increased as she watched Cross and Camilla become older, growing from babies, to teens, and then into new adults just starting their own lives. The fear grew because, as her babies got older, she found that she had less control, less contact, and less influence. She could no longer choose their playmates or watchers. They suddenly had social lives that did not include her. She had to rely on Cross and Camilla to do all the things for themselves to keep safe that had once been the responsibility of her and Calisto.

Emma wasn't sure her children could always do that.

Well …

At least, not as well as she did.

Still, Emma had done her best to step back, and hope for the best that she never had that call come in, or a visit.

And when it did finally come one warm, August night, Emma realized how entirely unprepared *she* had been for it. She raced to the hospital with her husband, where her son had been admitted, and found that she couldn't breathe. She was like a frozen statue, cold and unmoving, being shuffled from spot to spot while she waited for some kind of news about her nineteen year old son.

Unable to speak to ask her own questions, Emma opted to listen to the conversations happening around her instead. Calisto—always calm and in control no matter the situation—fielded questions and provided health information. He even went with a nurse to donate blood for their son in case more transfusions were needed.

Across from Emma in the family waiting room, sat a dishevelled, stunned eighteen year old Catherine Marcello. Emma still didn't know what had happened to her son, but she certainly couldn't be surprised to find out that Catherine had been with Cross during the event.

The two had been on again, off again from the beginning of their very early teen years. Sometimes, the two were more off than on. But for the last year, while Catherine began her first year of university, the two had been very much on, as far as Emma knew. The two shared a very expensive penthouse that

Cross owned in Manhattan, although Emma found that Catherine was rarely around whenever she visited her son.

Sometimes, it was hard to know what was going on, because Cross kept his personal life very quiet and private. He had always been like that, Emma thought, likely because Calisto had warned their son not to make a spectacle out of the women he chose to date or otherwise. Occasionally, Cross brought Catherine over to his parents' home to have dinner, but that was really the extent of Emma's interaction with the young woman.

At the same time, Cross had never brought *any* women home to meet his parents. He'd never mentioned any woman he was dating, not even in an off-handed manner, except for Catherine.

It was almost as if her son didn't think any woman was worth his time or effort to meet his family, or for him to talk about.

None, that was, except for Catherine Marcello.

Nearly a half of a decade of an on again, off again relationship. All that time of Emma only being able to name one girl her son had been seriously involved with.

In that moment, Emma did a double-take of Catherine.

The young woman was quite beautiful, as she had always been. She held a striking resemblance to her red-headed mother, yet had taken her father's vivid green eyes and brown hair. Emma certainly didn't wonder why the young woman had caught her son's eye. She was a beauty; a proper Italian beauty, with her olive complexion and sweet smile. But it was what was *beyond* the physical appearance that made Emma curious.

What was inside Catherine's mind and heart?

Were those the things that kept Cross running back to Catherine time and time again?

Were those unknown things what her son loved about Catherine Marcello?

Were those what *made* him love the girl?

Emma didn't know.

And that bothered her.

Emma readied to speak to Catherine, but didn't get a chance to say a word before a whole new group of people flooded the waiting room, loud and worried. Marcello people. Catherine's parents. An aunt, and an uncle or two.

Emma decided to stay in her seat as the young woman was surrounded by her family, their concerns and questions spilling out one right after the other.

"What happened?" Catrina, her mother, asked.

"Are you okay, *dolcezza*?" came the concern of her father, Dante.

The others managed to get their questions in, too. For the most part, Catherine stayed quiet, her gaze stuck on the doors where the doctors and nurses kept coming and going from. None had come to give any updates on Cross's condition, and the one time they had, Calisto had left with a nurse to donate blood.

He was a perfect match for Cross, after all, being his father. Even if the rest of the world didn't know it.

"Catherine," the girl's father said, "I need you to talk to me."

"I don't ... know," Catherine mumbled.

Dante frowned, and took a seat next to his daughter. "You were going to that party, right?"

Catherine nodded. "Yeah."

"Something happened there?"

Again, another nod.

Dante attempted to probe his daughter for more information, but continued to come up with little to nothing in response. Eventually, the girl's mother stepped in.

"Come on, Dante, let's step outside for a minute."

It wasn't long before the Marcello family cleared out of the waiting room. A few others followed. Calisto's men, likely, wanting to talk to Dante. It didn't leave Emma and Catherine entirely alone, but the few people left were huddled in the corner, involved in a quiet conversation.

"I'm sorry," Catherine whispered.

Emma glanced up at the young woman. "Pardon?"

Catherine repeated her apology, but Emma still didn't have a clue what the girl was actually apologizing for.

"I can't explain to them what happened," Catherine said with a shake of her head. "We weren't even where I told them I was going. It wasn't Cross's fault, not really."

Emma's brow furrowed. "You didn't go to a party, then?"

Cross was nineteen, which meant he didn't report to his parents regarding his whereabouts and what he did or didn't do. Maybe he did report to Calisto, occasionally, but certainly not to Emma.

"Not a party," Catherine admitted. "There was some things going on, a fight he wanted to see, and a race after. I wandered off when he was talking to somebody. I shouldn't have wandered off, not without Cross."

Emma was not a stupid woman, and she didn't live with her head stuck in the sand, either. She was well aware that Cross, like his father, dabbled in the illegal side of life and business more often than not. She understood perfectly well that there were plenty of things that Catherine probably wasn't saying.

It was a part of their life.

It was a part of being a woman involved with those kind of men.

And Catherine, like Emma, had grown up in that

life.

"You wandered off," Emma heard herself say faintly.

Catherine nodded, and wiped at her eyes with the heel of her palms. "Some creep cornered me, and then another one came out of fucking nowhere."

Emma cringed, her heart squeezing painfully. "Oh, sweetheart."

"Cross came out of nowhere, too. He got a hold of the one; I thought he was going to kill him."

"But?"

"I only saw the knife when it was too late," Catherine mumbled.

Emma blinked, finally understanding, finally *knowing*. She wished that knowing why and how lessened her anxiety, but it didn't.

"I'm so sorry," Catherine said for a third time. "I shouldn't have wandered off."

For a long while, Emma simply sat in silence, unsure of what to say. Catherine was the one to speak again first.

"I just ... they'll be so angry that I was with Cross when he was working and—"

"I get it," Emma interrupted. "But the bare bones of the story, your parents should know."

Catherine shrugged. "Yeah, probably."

"And Cross …" Emma trailed off, meeting Catherine's watery gaze. "Well, he's Cross."

A small smile lit up Catherine's features. "Yeah, he is."

That smile, and Catherine's quiet understanding of Emma's vague statement about her son said a hell of a lot more than the young girl possibly could on her own. Probably more than even Cross could, too. At least where her son's private relationship with Catherine was concerned.

Emma didn't need to explain to Catherine about Cross, because she already knew.

Knew that he was strong.

Knew that he was stubborn.

Knew that he would be okay.

And that knowledge, that deep, hidden understanding, didn't simply *show up* one day. It took real love to know someone so well, that all you needed was to hear their name to feel it in your soul.

Emma knew that kind of love.

And it was fucking terrifying.

"Ma?"

Cross's tired murmur broke Emma from her daze. She stopped her tinkering with the hospital room's blinds, and looked over at her son. Propped up in the bed, wearing one of his charming, disarming smiles, Cross sighed.

He'd been awake for a while, but not in the mood to talk. The nurse that had come in earlier to change the bandages on his left side had gotten a taste of the rare Donati attitude. Something that rarely reared its ugly head, especially with Cross.

Emma figured she could attribute that attitude to the deep stab wound in Cross's side that had nicked a vein and a kidney. Not to mention the fact that Cross continued to refuse any sort of pain medication for relief.

"You're looking happier," Emma said.

Cross shrugged. "If you say so. Where's Cal?"

As Cross had gotten older, he'd varied between calling Calisto his dad, papa, or simply Cal. Sometimes, it depended on his mood, and other times, who was around.

"He went out to grab me some lunch," Emma said.

Emma continued closing the blinds, needing something to do with her hands. Anything to keep her mind occupied.

"Ma."

Emma stilled again. "Yeah?"

"Stop fretting."

"I'm not. I'm—"

"Fretting," Cross muttered. "I'm okay, Ma."

"*Now*," Emma stressed, "Now you're okay, Cross."

"I've been okay for two days, actually. Release is in my very near future." Cross grinned, but it didn't help Emma's anxiety. "Please stop fretting, Ma."

Emma's arms fell limply to her sides, and she had all she could do to stop herself from crushing Cross in a hug. *Another* hug, because she had done that many times already. Her nineteen year old son had *not* been impressed.

"You don't understand, baby." And then, quickly, before Cross could give her one of his looks for calling him a baby, Emma added, "And I know you're not a baby, Cross. You're a young man, but you can be fifteen, or fifty, and you will still be my baby. So it's not that easy for me not to fret, as you say."

Emma blew out a breath, glancing at the hospital room doors and wondering where her husband was. He should have been back by now. "I spent so many years teaching you not to do unsafe things; don't run with scissors, don't climb too high. Be smart, make good decisions. And Calisto, he's done that with you, too."

"I know," Cross said.

"We do that because we live anxiously now, waiting and not wanting a phone call like we got the other night."

"Ma—"

"So no, I'm sorry to say it's not as simple as me stopping the fretting, Cross. And if it bothers you that

I worry, or that I haven't given you five minutes to breathe, then tough shit."

Her son's eyes widened, but he didn't say a word.

"I'm your mother. I spent thirty-two weeks carrying you before I brought you into this world. Thirty-two weeks that nearly killed me for more reasons than you will ever know. Now, I have loved you for every single day of your nineteen years. I have fed you, cleaned you, rocked you to sleep, and let you grow. You were the one to put me through that phone call I never wanted to get. You can deal with my *fretting*."

Cross nodded once.

Smart man.

"You got it, Ma."

"Good."

Emma moved closer to Cross, patted his bruised cheek softly with her palm, and then stepped back from him just as quickly.

"I'm sorry for scaring you, Ma," he said softly.

"Say it a few more times, and a little louder for the people in the back."

Cross chuckled. "Milk it up, Ma."

"Oh, I plan to."

Emma went back to flitting around the room, moving papers and distracting herself.

"But I would do it again," Cross said suddenly, "and I'm not sorry for that, Ma."

Emma froze at those words.

She had watched Catherine Marcello come and go, come and go, and come and go some more from Cross's room. It was the only moments when Emma allowed herself to leave her son in peace and privacy.

"I know you would," Emma said.

"Do you?" her son asked.

She turned to face him.

"*L'amore é forte come la morte.* Love is strong—like death," Emma murmured. "It almost makes love sound grim, or morbid even, but ..."

"That's because it's true."

Emma shrugged helplessly. "They are the only two things in life that have nearly the same profound effect on us all. Like without love, death is near. And with love, we might not mind death *for* love. I just didn't realize it until the other night that perhaps you did love Catherine. You're always so quiet about her, and *that*."

Cross smiled. "Of course I love her, Ma. I have always loved her. I always will, even if she doesn't love me."

That, Emma understood, too.

9.
DONATI
UNSEEN FILES #5

Camilla + Tommaso

"Hey, uh, boss. Could I chat with you for a minute?"

The unfamiliar voice made Calisto look up from the paperwork on his desk. It wasn't often he chose to work outside of his home, but sometimes a change of venue was a good thing. It kept him on his toes.

He expected to see one of the restaurant workers in the doorway, but that was not who he found.

"Tommaso," Calisto said, surprised to see the twenty-one year old Chicago Outfit *principe* standing in his business. "I heard you were in town."

"Dad thought I needed a break."

"We all do occasionally. How is your father?"

"He's Tommas Rossi. How do you think?"

Calisto laughed. "As thick-headed and stubborn as ever, then."

"He can be. So do you have that minute, or ...?"

"Come on in. Close the door."

Tommaso did as he was told, and Calisto took the moment he had to give the young man another once-over. It had been two years since the last time he had seen Tommaso. Calisto had been on a business trip to Chicago, and Tommaso was celebrating his nineteenth birthday.

As far as Calisto knew, Tommaso had made friends with the Marcello family in New York while traveling with his father, a boss of another criminal organization. And since Calisto's son, Cross, often hung around with Andino Marcello, he and Tommaso had struck up a friendship as well.

Calisto never stepped in to stop Cross from making friends, connections, or allies within other families and organizations. It would only benefit his son in the future to have those contacts should he need them.

Cross made those friendships organically—

without help—which Calisto considered another benefit to his son's disarming charm.

But, Tommaso didn't have a lot of connection to Calisto. Certainly not enough to be seeking him out for a private conversation at a restaurant without some kind of prior notice.

"Cross told me where I could find you today," Tommaso said as he took a seat across from the desk.

"I wondered how you found me. Now, I'm more curious as to *why*."

Tommaso smiled, but there was still a nervous aura surrounding the young man. Like the way he shifted in the chair, kept his hands stuffed in his pockets, or wouldn't meet Calisto's gaze for too long.

"Shit," Calisto said. "Please don't tell me you killed one of my guys, or some nonsense like that."

That broke the tension long enough for Tommaso to laugh, and lean back in the chair. It didn't last for too long, though. Just as quickly, Tommaso sobered and straightened fully. "No, nothing like that. But you know, depending on how this goes, make sure to tell my mother that I love her, and all that good shit."

Calisto's brow furrowed, and he decided it was time to stop messing around. He put away his papers, shut down his laptop, and gave Tommaso his full attention.

"All right," Calisto said, "give me the bad news, whatever it is."

"Not that, either." Tommaso sighed. "It's just … I'm not used to needing to approach a girl's father, you know? I don't normally have to do that being who I am, and who my father is. Except you're not like other men, you're like my father, but here, in New York. And if someone approached my sister before they went to Tommas—"

"Back the fuck up," Calisto interrupted.

Tommaso glanced up. "Huh?"

"This is about Camilla?" Calisto asked, confused. "You're here about my daughter?"

"Uh, yeah?"

"Well, don't fucking pose it as a question, now. Either you are, or you are not. Which one is it?"

Tommaso cleared his throat. "I am."

Well.

Huh.

Calisto felt about as shocked as Tommaso looked in that moment. He certainly understood *why* the young man felt so shook up, however …

"Sorry, but you just came here for nothing, Tommaso."

"Pardon?"

"You wasted your time," Calisto clarified, "especially coming to me."

"That has got to be the fastest rejection—"

"No." Calisto rubbed a spot on his forehead where tension was beginning to irritate him. "I mean, I take it you're here to ask me if you can take my daughter out, and you don't need to ask *me* at all. I don't make those choices for Cam, I never have. Neither does her mother. She's nineteen, smart as fuck, too; so she is more than capable of saying whether or not she's interested in someone."

Tommaso rested back in his chair. "But you're …"

"For Camilla? I'm just her dad. And I love her very much. So, should something happen between the two of you that displeases me because it displeases her, then you can safely assume we will revisit this conversation."

Calisto smiled, adding, "But until then, Tommaso, the rest is up to, and has always been up to, my daughter."

"Okay."

Calisto waved at his office door, dismissing his guest. "So, have a nice day, and enjoy your visit. If it helps with Cam, she likes action movies, pretty cars, and dancing."

But Calisto didn't know if that would help Tommaso all that much. Camilla was different than other girls her age.

Different and difficult and wonderful.

She didn't make time for boys, not in any serious manner. She almost saw them as commodities in her life. Once she was bored, she moved on. Calisto wasn't sure if that was because Camilla had yet to meet the right guy, or she wasn't all that interested in meeting him at all.

Nonetheless, Calisto's position remained the same.

It would always be his daughter's choice.

He had no say.

With a quick goodbye, Tommaso was gone from Calisto's office, leaving him alone to his work and thoughts once again. He let out a breath, wondering how he wanted—or should—feel regarding what just happened.

He didn't entirely know.

He supposed it was all on Tommaso, now.

Calisto wished him luck.

"Emma!"

"Hmm?"

His wife barely reacted to his sharp whisper. Calisto was *trying* to be discreet, but his distracted wife was not helping the situation. Emma bounced from one thing to the other in the kitchen, doing what she did best.

"Emma!" Calisto whisper-hissed again.

"What, Cal? Can't you see that I'm busy?"

Finally, his wife glanced up at him, her gaze

narrowed. Now, usually, Calisto would take that as a clear sign of Emma's irritation with him and book it the hell out of there as fast as he could. He couldn't do that this time.

"Someone is here," Calisto said from the kitchen entryway.

Emma simply stared at him like he had grown a second head. "We're having a *dinner*. Yes, people are coming over."

Calisto shook his head. "No."

"Well, it's a bit late for you to be refusing now. People are already here, or so you said."

He had the strangest urge to smack his head against the nearest wall. "Emma, listen to me for five seconds."

"I am. You're the one acting like a bee crawled up your ass or something."

"Someone is here," Calisto repeated, this time adding, "*with* Camilla."

Emma instantly stopped what she was doing. "What?"

"Yes, that's what I said."

"But—"

Calisto heard two distinct sets of footsteps approaching from behind; one familiar, and the other, not so much. He gave his wife a look, and then stepped aside as the two people came closer.

Camilla walked into the kitchen with a wide smile. Tommaso Rossi followed right behind her. Calisto's gaze dropped to the two's connected hands, and it seemed he wasn't the only one to notice. Emma glanced down to see the affection between the two, as well, but she didn't hide her surprise nearly as well as Calisto did.

"Oh," Emma mumbled. "Well, hello."

Calisto almost laughed.

Almost.

He had no idea how he managed to hold it back, but he did. It certainly was a shock to see their daughter bring someone to a family dinner. As a *date*. It was even more surprising to see her date be Tommaso Rossi.

"You don't mind putting an extra plate on the table, right, Ma?" Camilla asked.

Emma recovered from her shock beautifully. As she always did. It was one of the things—many things—that Calisto loved about his wife.

"Yes, of course," Emma told their daughter. "So, do you want to introduce us properly, or …?" Emma trailed off with an exaggerated nod in Tommaso's direction. The young man only chuckled. "I mean, if you want to."

She knew damn well who Tommaso was. Calisto had told his wife about him *six fucking months* ago when Tommaso had approached him about Camilla. Of course, Calisto hadn't heard much about his daughter or Tommaso after that, and he knew the young man had eventually headed back to Chicago. It was, after all, where Tommaso's life and family happened to be.

Calisto assumed that was the end of it.

Apparently not.

"Ma, Daddy," Camilla said with a roll of her eyes, "This is Tommaso. He made a special trip down from Chicago to see me. Since I was already having dinner here tonight, I figured he could join me."

Emma nodded. "Okay. Hello, Tommaso."

"A special trip?" Calisto asked.

He ignored the look his wife shot him.

"I kind of missed New York," Tommaso said, smiling at Camilla.

Yeah.

Calisto thought it was more likely *someone* in New York.

Someone like Camilla.

"Huh," Calisto said.

"All right," Camilla jumped in, giving her father a side-eye that could rival her mother's. "We are going to take a walk through the back property until dinner is ready. Shoot me a text, in case we're too far to hear you yell, Ma."

"Sure," Emma replied. "I can do that."

The two young adults wasted no time getting out of the kitchen, still connected by their hands the entire time. Calisto waited an extra few minutes, just to be sure they were out of earshot, before he turned back to his wife, knowing she had a million and one things to say to him.

"A little bit of a warning would have been nice, Cal," Emma said.

"I tried," Calisto argued.

Emma turned to look out the window in the

kitchen that faced the large backyard, and showcased where the property melted into a line of trees and trails. There, Calisto could see Camilla and Tommaso heading for one of the trails that would lead to a little pond and sitting area.

"Wasn't that like six months ago when he was here last?"

"Yep," Calisto said.

"Huh."

"Yep."

He wasn't entirely sure how to feel about it, either.

"Well," Emma drawled under her breath.

"He's good, as far as that goes," Calisto said, more for himself than his wife. "He comes from a good man, so that's a bonus."

"Well."

"Spit it out, Emma."

"Maybe that is the trick to Camilla."

"I don't understand."

"Cam," Emma said, "and boys. You know how she is. They don't keep her interest longer than a toy does for a toddler. Maybe he figured out a way around that with her."

"And how would that be?"

"Distance and space," Emma offered with a shrug. "One thing at a time, maybe."

"Emmy, love, no man has the sort of patience needed for that kind of shit."

Emma looked over her shoulder at Calisto, her expression both soft and serious at the same time. "Really?"

"What?"

"If he loved her, even if it's crazy to love someone else that fast and *know* you do, then would patience and time matter if you got what you wanted in the end?"

"I hadn't thought about that," Calisto replied.

"You've got time. Think about it now."

Calisto did. It seemed he might not have given Tommaso enough credit all those months ago.

"Well, then."

Emma smiled. "As long as she's happy."

Yes, that, too.

DONATI
OTHER POV FILES

10.
DONATI
OTHER POV FILES #1

Affonso Donati

Affonso Donati wondered as he watched a young couple lean closer at a nearby table, their hands touching and eyes never leaving one another, if he could possibly understand that sort of emotional devotion to another person. That complete, pure type of loyalty and love that would make him want to bring a woman constantly, impossibly closer. A feeling that would have him always needing to touch her, and then still have him running back for more, later.

He didn't wonder for long.

Affonso didn't understand those sorts of nuances between lovers at all. He never had, despite his two decade long marriage, not to mention his many dalliances with women and mistresses over the years. He fully expected, and believed, that he would never truly understand those strange things.

Perhaps he was just incapable.

Who was to say?

The closest thing he had ever come to that sort of deep emotion was an obsession with Camilla Calisto Donati during his younger years, but even that hadn't been a proper love. And it ended terribly, for both of them.

Affonso supposed his raising probably had a great deal to do with all of his perspective, or lack thereof, on the matter. A philandering father who made no secret of his constant affairs with many women, and a mother who never spoke against her husband's choices. His father had always kept a handful of whores on the side to feed his whims, and often brought his two sons along for the ride.

On the other hand, Affonso's mother was the perfect housewife incarnate, always presentable and respectable. Her children were always clean and well-behaved. Food was always on the table for each meal of the day, never failing. Her children were seen, but never heard. And Affonso had never heard his mother complain about any of it, even when she was sick.

Affonso had learned, through years of watching the dynamics between his parents, that this too was the type of relationship he wanted—*expected*—between himself and his wife. It seemed normal enough, the way his father never hid his intentions or affairs from his wife, and how his mother simply bent to her husband's whims.

Had she been unhappy, surely she would have spoken up?

Had she been in pain, surely her sons would have seen it?

Affonso remembered nothing of the sort from his mother. And so, he fully believed that all women were capable of behaving in the same way. But if they struggled, he also figured they could learn what was expected of them over time. After all, falling in line was much easier than being constantly unhappy.

Like anything else in life, this too could be learned.

His first wife had been perfect, or as near to it as a woman could be. Her own raising, one similar to Affonso's, had likely helped her along a great deal in that respect. She birthed him children, kept his home clean and beautiful, warmed his bed when he wanted her to, and she turned her cheek to his affairs and business dealings over the years. She was quite happy to just be and be let be, so to speak.

She had been happy in her place, and satisfied by material things instead of emotional nonsense and empty promises of fidelity that Affonso could not keep.

The only thing his wife had never done that he wished for, was birth him a son. Two healthy girls, sure, but never a boy to carry on his name and legacy. Oh, there had been the stillborn son at seven months gestation …

Affonso shook the thought away.

He did not think about that.

He would not.

That event had happened just a year into their marriage. He could not remember a more devastating event in his life emotionally. Back in those times, fathers had been expected to stay at home or in the waiting room until birth was over. Affonso had demanded to be present for the birth. It was his first child with his wife, after all.

They knew the baby was a bit early.

They had not known he would be dead.

"A boy," the doctor had whispered into the quiet delivery room.

Too quiet.

Affonso distinctly remembered the elation in his heart at hearing those two words. A boy. His boy. And then as fast as that joy had come into his heart, it was violently ripped away. Slippery, wet, and bloodstained, the baby came into the world *silent*. And blue on his lips, one little hand clenched into a fist, and the other spread wide open. Ten fingers, and ten toes. Perfect features that seemed oh, so still.

He was doll-like.

The baby boy never breathed.

He never moved or opened his eyes.

He never lived.

He never *was*.

Devastating wasn't a good enough word, but it

was the best one Affonso had.

It was the only memory in Affonso's life that he willingly chose to supress with every bit of effort he could bring forth. It was the only time he had seen his wife cry.

Never again.

It could ruin a man. He was not made for that sort of pain.

No one is, he thought sadly as he watched the young couple just one table over. Sure, life was simple and easy for them now, or it appeared that way, but life would eventually teach them its terrible truths, too.

In time, it always did.

That was unavoidable.

"You seem distracted."

The statement of his companion brought Affonso out of his thoughts, and back to the meeting at hand. He was grateful for the reprieve.

"We could do this another time, if you prefer," Maximo said.

Affonso shook his head. "No, old friend. Now is perfectly fine. I was just thinking about my deceased wife, that's all."

Maximo's expression softened. "Ah, well, if you're not ready to discuss this arrangement, then I can certainly understand why."

Affonso regarded his counterpart for a moment, wondering how similar yet different the two were in the grand scheme of things. Both men were respected bosses of their Cosa Nostra families. Affonso in New York, and Maximo Sorrento in Las Vegas.

But that was just about where the similarities ended.

"You know," Affonso started to say, "At my age, I'm not required to go through this charade again. I was married for two decades, I'm nearing my sixties. It just isn't expected for a man—a boss—of my age and position to remarry to please the Commission."

Maximo nodded. "I'm aware. And yet, here you are, looking for another wife. A *young* wife, I might add. You even have the option to choose this time around, without the usual constraints and rules of made men to weigh down your choices. Except, you're still opting for the proper Catholic, Italian woman of a respectable house and name."

"I am," Affonso agreed.

"Why?"

"Unfinished business, I suppose."

"Oh?"

"A boy," Affonso murmured. "A son. I would like to have one to carry on my family's name and *my* legacy in this thing of ours. Doesn't every man in our position?"

"I see," Maximo said.

"My wife has been dead long enough, and so, it is time to move on."

"Then it's time to get to business, isn't it?"

Affonso smiled. "It is always time for business."

Maximo gestured over his shoulder, and quickly, one of his waiting men stepped forward, a file waiting in his hand. He passed the item over to his boss without a word, and Maximo then slid it across the restaurant table to Affonso.

Opening the file, Affonso found a photo of a beautiful blonde, green-eyed woman staring back at him. A young woman, yet not too young. She certainly didn't have a child-like appearance, but rather, a woman just stepping into adulthood and what it would bring to her life. She was perfectly put together. Impeccably dressed in beautiful clothes. Heathy-looking. Petite. Smiling brightly at the person taking the photo.

Emma Sorrento. Affonso took in the details of Maximo's niece that had been provided in the file of information. Her age, schooling, interests, and training. Piano and ballet, like his own daughters. She was perfect in a sense, everything that a mafia wife should be on the surface.

"You should know," Maximo started to say as Affonso continued flipping through the information and few pictures, "something about Emma."

"And what is that?"

"We've allowed her a degree of freedom in her life. It helps to keep her happy, if you understand—"

"With men, you mean?"

Maximo cleared his throat. "Well, yes, exactly that."

Affonso cared little for that information. "I don't mind."

"No?"

He almost laughed at the surprise in the other

man's voice. While he could certainly understand the appeal and desire a man would have for a virgin, it was not currently high in Affonso's personal needs or wants.

"I married a virgin once," Affonso admitted, shrugging. "And I spent the first six months of our marriage teaching her what to do. I'm not interested in teaching a woman how to please me, or herself, for that matter. I want a son, that's all, nothing more. I figure a woman who understands how to get herself in such a way will work better for me than one who knows nothing."

"You could be right," Maximo said.

Affonso closed the file and slid it back across the table. "I am never wrong, Maximo. I'll agree to a marriage with the girl. Soon."

11.
DONATI
OTHER POV FILES #2

Camilla Donati (Calisto's Mother)

Camilla Calisto remembered vividly the day she had met Richard Donati for the first time. The meeting had been stiff, awkward even, between the two. Still young enough not to care much for rules or demands, yet still old enough to understand what was happening and what was expected of her, it was bound to be … interesting.

She hadn't been ready to marry. And certainly *not* to a man she didn't know from Adam and Eve.

It also wasn't her choice to make. Or so her parents explained again and again. Nothing was her choice to make, apparently.

So, she had put on her party dress, brushed

mascara on her lashes, set her curls, and painted a perfect red smile on her lips. Camilla couldn't do a lot of things, but she did know how to be pretty.

Her mother always liked to say that pretty women never lost.

To his benefit, Richard Donati had not seemed particularly happy about that day, either. Like her, he had dressed for the day, but his interest was clearly elsewhere. Not that Camilla blamed him, what with everyone watching the two of them interact like they were some kind of alien pair.

It was always easier on the men than the woman where the mafia was concerned. There were different expectations set out between the two genders, lines that seemed to be polar opposites when it came to behavior, respect, and so much more.

Girls had to be everything good.

Boys only had to be very little.

She knew it was unfair.

She also didn't know any different.

So, when that meeting of their families had ended with a shiny new engagement ring on her finger, Camilla had done nothing more than smile and say thank you. After all, that was what a good *Mafioso principessa* did.

And she was good.

"You're tittering," Camilla's mother said.

"I'm nervous."

Camilla, not wanting to deal with her mother's hovering and droning on, shooed her out of the private room. Her makeup was already done, her hair had long been set, and her dress was on and buttoned up the back, so she simply didn't need her mother there.

Especially not if she was going to annoy her and make her nerves even worse. Even with her mother gone, Camilla couldn't manage to soothe her nerves.

Dammit.

When a knock echoed on the door, Camilla assumed it was just her mother trying to come back. Instead of checking first, she flung the door wide open with a huff. She was doing what her parents wanted and expected from her with this whole marriage and day. The least they could do for her was give her some privacy on her wedding day.

It wasn't her mother behind the door.

Richard, her very soon-to-be husband, stood there, his eyes wide and a smile already starting to form. He had his hands shoved into the pockets of his tux pants. Camilla was struck silent by how handsome he looked, all dressed up and *happy*.

"Oh," Camilla said softly.

Richard shot her a sly smile. "Sorry. I thought your mother would be here with you, and that she would answer the door. I wanted to bring you a little gift before the ceremony started."

It took Camilla far too long to find her voice again. "I kicked her out."

"Why?"

"She wouldn't leave me alone. I couldn't breathe with her hovering."

Richard nodded. "That seems like a perfectly reasonable reason."

"Are you patronizing me?"

He laughed. "No, not at all."

Then, Camilla had another realization. She gasped, horrified at her stupid mistake. "Oh, my God. My dress; you're not supposed to see it or be here! Get out!"

She tried to close the door, but he blocked her effort with one strong arm, and another one of his goddamn laughs. "A little late now, isn't it?"

"It's bad luck!"

"Nonsense, Camilla. And you look beautiful, by the way."

Camilla stopped trying to shut the door in Richard's face, taken aback by the freely offered compliment. "Do I?"

"Yes, very beautiful. Hasn't anyone stopped moving long enough today to tell you that?"

"My mother, but I don't think she really counts."

"What about your father?"

"He hasn't been around to chat yet," she admitted.

Richard shook his head. "Well, that's a goddamn shame. Everyone should be telling you. It's your day."

"Funny, it feels more like my—or *our*—parents'

day."

He shrugged. "They're not the ones who get to have all the fun tonight, though."

Camilla felt her cheeks heat up at his blatant suggestion. "Stop that."

"Why, is that what has gotten you all worked up today? *Sex*?"

"Okay, you can go now."

Richard didn't move a single inch. "Cam, sex is the last thing you should be worried about, I promise."

"Says you. You have had all the time in the world to run around with whoever the hell you wanted, sleeping with all of them, for all I know. And me? Not the same. *At all.*"

"That still makes literally no difference to what I said, though."

"According to you," she muttered heavily.

Richard smiled a slow and sinful sight. "Well, I suppose you're just going to have to trust me, huh?"

Camilla rolled her eyes. "That is a lot of faith to give to a man who hasn't done more than hold my hand, or kiss my cheek. We haven't even kissed properly! And tonight, you want me to just—"

"All right. That's quite enough. You're working yourself into a fit for nothing at all."

"Nothing?" she screeched.

Richard let out another dark laugh before he leaned further into the doorway, and kissed Camilla softly on her lips. It stopped her crazy thoughts, her running mouth, and all her worries in one fell swoop. She expected Richard to pull away, but he didn't. Instead, he moved a little closer, his hands gripping tight to her trim waist to pull her into him. His tongue teased the seam of her lips, and Camilla opened her mouth to his silent request.

Kissing wasn't so hard or strange, she found.

Natural.

Instinctive.

Richard led, she followed suit.

He made it easy.

And sweet.

Maybe … maybe sex would be the same.

As Richard finally pulled away from the kiss, he stroked Camilla's cheeks with his thumbs. His smile had softened, and her nerves were practically all but gone.

"See," he said thickly, "nothing to worry about."

Was it normal to have no air after a kiss?

Camilla didn't know.

"You'll always be like that … easy?" she dared to ask.

"And slow. Whatever you need, Cam. The only thing you don't need to do, is worry."

"Okay."

"Now, your gift."

She had forgotten about that. His reason for being there at all when he wasn't supposed to be.

Richard pulled a hand-sized box from his pocket. Soft, black velvet slid into Camilla's palm before he opened it up. Inside, a delicate gold necklace waited, resting atop more velvet. Hanging from the chain were a set of small, golden piano keys.

Camilla smiled widely. She loved the piano, and so did Richard. She was not nearly as good as he was, but she had learned more from him in just a few months than she ever had under a formal teacher. It was how he had broken through some of her walls leading up to their arranged wedding, by playing for her and teaching her.

"The keys can be engraved, too," Richard said, turning the piano keys over under his fingers. There, on one, their wedding date was inscribed. "I thought we could add more dates, and more keys, if we need to as time goes on."

It was perfect.

He didn't have to do this at all, and yet, he had.

"Thank you," was all she managed to say.

"I'll meet you at the end, Cam."

I'll meet you at the end, Cam.

Those words haunted Camilla, now.

She stared at the headstone bearing her dead husband's name and date of death. She didn't visit Richard's grave very often, but sometimes, unknown forces drove her to him, and she talked for hours, not knowing if he was listening or not.

Their marriage had not been easy for a multitude

of reasons. She was young, difficult, and stubborn. He was firm, quiet, and had a taste for free women.

But he had treated her well, too. He had never hit her, never hurt her physically. And though it took a while, she did come to love Richard in her own way.

And then he was taken away.

The gentle kicks of her unborn baby drew her mind from the haze of sadness. Camilla rubbed a hand over her nearly nine-month swell. Any day now, and the child would make his or her way into the world.

But the baby would never know, she decided. The baby *would never* know the truth, if she could help it. Even with him dead, Camilla would rather Richard be seen as the child's father as opposed to the horrible truth.

Because the truth was a monster.

And no baby deserved that.

"Camilla?" Affonso called from the edge of the cemetery. "Are you ready?"

How nice Affonso had seemed.

How sweet and caring.

How could a rapist hide his monsters so well?

"I'm coming, Affonso."

AUTHOR'S NOTE

This is the end of *Behind the Bloodlines*, and I certainly hoped the readers enjoyed this extra content for the *Trilogy*. I chose to end this bonus content novella with Camilla, Calisto's mother, because it felt full circle for the story. Where the secrets first began, where the bloodlines started to tell lies and hide truths ... with Camilla, and an almost-born Calisto.

Hugs, my lovely readers, there is more yet to come.

There is always more yet to come.

—Kris

ABOUT THE AUTHOR

Bethany-Kris is a Canadian author, lover of much, and mother to three very young sons, one cat, and two dogs. A small town in Eastern Canada where she was born and raised is where she has always called home. With her boys under her feet, a snuggling cat, barking dogs, and a spouse calling over his shoulder, she is nearly always writing something ... when she can find the time.

Find Bethany-Kris at:
Her website www.bethanykris.com,
or on Facebook at
www.facebook.com/bethanykriswrites,
on her blog at www.bethanykris.com/blog,
or on Twitter - @BethanyKris.

Sign up to Bethany-Kris's New Release Newsletter here: http://eepurl.com/bf9lzD

OTHER BOOKS

Cross + Catherine

Always
Revere (Coming Soon)

Guzzi Duet

Unraveled
Entangled

DeLuca Duet

Waste of Worth: Part One
Worth of Waste: Part Two

Standalone Titles

Inflict

Filthy Marcellos

Antony
Lucian
Giovanni
Dante
Legacy
The Complete Collection

The Chicago War

Deathless & Divided
Reckless & Ruined
Scarless & Sacred
Breathless & Bloodstained

Gun Moll Trilogy

Gun Moll
Gangster Moll
Madame Moll (Coming Soon)

Seasons of Betrayal

Where the Sun Hides
Where the Snow Falls
Where the Wind Whispers

BEHIND THE BLOODLINES

Donati Bloodlines

Thin Lies
Thin Lines
Thin Lives
Donati Bloodlines: The Complete Trilogy

The Russian Guns

The Arrangement
The Life
The Score
Demyan & Ana
Shattered
The Jersey Vignettes

Find more on Bethany-Kris's website at
www.bethanykris.com.